ZARBI

AND THE FIRE BREATHING DRAGON

Iker Burguera

First Printing: 2014

ISBN-13: 978-1505266214
ISBN-10: 1505266211

Aizkorri Kalea N24 5-D
Legazpi, Gipuzkoa 20230
Spain

http://www.arbitheaugmentedrealitybook.com/

Buy this book on the Web

For Bookstores, Wholesalers and further details please contact the publisher at the web page or in the following address:
ikerburguera@gmail.com

AUTHORS INFORMATION

- Author: Iker Burguera

- Illustrator: Tony Ganem

- Story: Emma Flemming and Iker Burguera

- Augmented Reality and Software Development: Iker Burguera and Vuforia Qualcomm

DEDICATION

To my family and friends, keep your dreams alive.

Understand that to achieve anything in life requires faith and belief in yourself, vision, hard work, determination, and dedication. Indeed, this book is dedicated to those people.

Enjoy ;)

INSTRUCTIONS

1

DOWNLOAD THE BOOK APP "ARBI" FROM:

2

POINT THE CAMERA TO THE IMAGES ON THE BOOK

3

ENJOY !!

Once upon a time in a beautiful valley far, far away was a peaceful village. Everything and everyone lived in perfect harmony. The friendly villagers were always happy and full of smiles.

Until one day...

A fierce fire breathing dragon flew across the sky high above the village. As it roared, flames shot out its mouth. The dragon flapped its wings, soared even higher into the sky and then landed on the top of a nearby mountain. At the top of the mountain was a deep, dark cave that the dragon wanted to use as its lair.

The dragon saw the happy villagers living together in harmony. He was jealous. "I will burn down your village!" he roared. The villagers were terrified! "What shall we do? Who can help us?" they cried.

The villagers ran for help to the brave knight Arbi.

Arbi lived in a small castle just outside the village. He was famous for having defeated many monsters. The villagers knew that if anyone could help save them, this brave knight could. Arbi wanted to save the village, but his sword couldn't beat a fire breathing dragon.

Arbi went to ask his friend Smarlow the tortoise for advice, he was a very smart tortoise. Smarlow gave the brave knight a magic potion. "Use this magic potion to put out the dragon's fire. You'll need to pour the potion into his mouth. I am too slow to fight the dragon myself so you must find a brave team to help you."

Arbi went to find Agick the cat. "Agick, you are

so agile and so quick. Can you help me pour this

potion into the dragon's mouth?"

"Of course I will help," said Agick.

Arbi and Agick realised that they would not be able to find the dragon's lair in the thick forest on the mountain. "What shall we do? How will we be able to track down the dragon?"

"Eureka! I know! Let's ask Smellit the dog to help us. He can sniff out the dragon's trail for us!"

Arbi and Agick went to ask Smellit for his help.

"Smellit, please can you help us track down the dragon?" they asked.

"Of course I will help you guys" said Smellit.

The three friends waved goodbye to Smarlow and set off to find the dragon. Smellit sniffed the dragon's smoke all the way to his lair. Would the three friends be able to defeat the dragon?

The dragon roared, "Grrrrrrrraaaaaaaaarrrgh!" Fire shot out his mouth. Arbi took out his sword but the flames were too big and too hot for the knight to get anywhere near the dragon. Smellit could see that they were in trouble.

"None of us can defeat the dragon on our own," said Arbi, "but maybe if we work together as a team we can save our village."

Suddenly, Smellit ran and bit the dragon's tail. The dragon got such a fright that he turned around with his mouth wide open. This was just what Agick had been waiting for! "Come on, Agick, you can do it! This is our chance to beat the dragon!" cried Arbi. Agick swiftly climbed a tree and quickly poured the magic potion into the dragon's mouth.

The dragon opened his mouth to roar, but there was no fire. Instead, thick dark smoke filled the sky. The potion had worked! The dragon's fire is gone!

"Hurray!" shouted Agick.

"Yay! The dragon is defeated!" shouted Smellit.

I couldn't have done this alone. Thank you for your help and teamwork," said Arbi.

As the three friends started walking back to the village, Arbi looked behind him and saw that the dragon looked very sad. They turned around went back to the dragon's lair.

"Dragon, why did you want to burn down our village?" asked Arbi.

"I was jealous of your happiness," said the dragon.

"You should be our friend, then you can be happy too," said Agick.

"I know! You can help us by protecting the village!" said Smellit.

"But how? I can't breathe fire anymore," said the dragon.

"Wait here, I have a plan," said Arbi.

The brave knight ran back to the village to find Smarlow the tortoise.

"Smarlow, please can you help me? Our new friend the dragon needs our help. Please can you give me an antidote?"

Smarlow gave Arbi another magic potion for the dragon.

Arbi and Smarlow went back up the mountain to meet Agick, Smellit and the defeated dragon.

"Dragon, will you be our friend and help us by protecting our village?" asked Arbi.

"Of course! I will be happy to protect my new friends," said the dragon. "I don't want to be jealous any more. I want to live in harmony with the village."

"Here, take this bottle and drink the magic potion," said Arbi. "This will give you back your fire, but you will only be able to use your fire for good deeds."

The dragon drank the magic potion. As the

happiness filled his body, his scales changed colour.

He used his new fire to provide light so that they

could find their way back to the village through

the forest.

The four friends returned to the village and told

the villagers that the dragon was their friend and

protector. The villagers cheered and celebrated

for weeks. The villagers and the dragon lived

together in harmony, happily ever after.

THE END

ABOUT THE AUTHOR

 Iker Burguera was born in Legazpi, a small town located in the Basque Country in 1986. He has been interested in Electronics and Engineering since childhood and soon became interested in programming. He holds a degree in Telecommunication Engineering at Mondragon University and a Master Thesis in Linköping University, Sweden. As a passionate of Electronics and Open Source movement, teaches and contributes to Arduino and Raspberry Pi community. He specializes on Project Management, Electronics and Software Development. He loves new challenges and enjoys his free time biking with friends and creating and developing new technology stuff.

Made in the USA
Charleston, SC
18 May 2015